MY AWFUL COUSIN
NORBERT

MY AWFUL COUSIN NORBERT

by BEVERLY KELLER
illustrated by BOBBY LEWIS

Lothrop, Lee & Shepard Books
New York

First Edition
1 2 3 4 5 6 7 8 9 10

Library of Congress Cataloging in Publication Data
Keller, Beverly.
My awful cousin Norbert.
Summary: The success of Mother's important dinner for her boss is endangered
when Norbert is invited. [1. Family life—Fiction] I. Lewis, Bobby (date). II. Title.
PZ7.K2813My [E] 81-6068
ISBN 0-688-00742-2 AACR2 ISBN 0-688-00743-0 (lib. bdg.)

For Sara

"My boss is coming to dinner tonight,"
Mother told me.
"I invited your cousin Norbert over
so you won't have to eat
in the kitchen alone."

"You should never ask Norbert to dinner.
Every time he's around
I get in trouble," I said.

7

"Don't fuss at me, Phil," Mother warned.
"My boss is thinking of giving me
an important new job.
I want her to see I have taste,
and style,
and a civilized home life."

"When I get in trouble,
Norbert acts polite and respectful,
but when you're not looking,
he grins."
I tried to sound civilized.

"Don't argue with your mother, Philip."
My father was firm.
"She's already invited Norbert,
and that's that."

My parents rushed around
getting ready for Mother's boss.
Then my father made a lemon cream pie.
He claims his lemon cream pie
is the greatest in the world.
Sometimes I wish
he were as proud of me
as he is of his lemon cream pie.

When it was done,
my father held it up
as if it were an emperor's crown.
"Is that a work of art,
or is that a work of art?"

"It's perfect."
Mother shoved back all the jars and bottles
on the second shelf of the refrigerator.
"Absolutely perfect."

Were they ever
that excited about me?

Father put the pie on the shelf.
"Whatever you do, Phil,
don't touch it," he warned me.
"Don't even jiggle
the refrigerator door."

Was he ever
that careful with me?

Mother set the dining room table
with a white embroidered cloth
and matching napkins,
the best silver, flowers,
and tall white candles
in crystal holders.

She had me put plastic place mats,
old stainless-steel knives and forks,
paper napkins, and plastic glasses
on the kitchen table.
Then she made me take a bath
and put on good clothes,
even though I was going to eat
in the kitchen.

Norbert came over,
looking clean
and wearing a suit.
I guess my parents had told him
about Mother's boss.

The food Mother put in the oven
looked like the covers
on the magazines at the supermarket.
She also stuck in two frozen dinners.

When the doorbell rang,
she and my father hurried to the front door.

"Your mother walks like an ostrich,"
Norbert said.

I could hear voices in the entry hall.
Father came into the kitchen
and fixed drinks
and took them to the parlor
on a tray.

"Your father looks like
Laurel and Hardy in that suit,"
Norbert told me.

Mother returned
and picked up a tray of cheese.
"Come meet my boss, Mrs. Tree," she told us,
"and then stay out of the way."

Even sitting on the parlor sofa,
Mrs. Tree looked tall
and thin and fierce.
When Mother introduced us,
Mrs. Tree said, "How do you do,"
without smiling.
The small dog on her lap showed its teeth
and growled.

Mother herded Norbert and me
back to the kitchen.
Then she took the appetizers
from the refrigerator
to the dining room.

Father came in and took
the frozen dinners from the oven
and set them on the table.
"There you go, boys."
He went back to the dining room.

Norbert sat at the kitchen table.
"That old Mrs. Tree is weird,
bringing a creepy dog with her."

"*Shh.*" I glanced at the
dining room door.
Mrs. Tree had looked at us
as if she knew every awful thing
we had ever thought.

"*Shh . . . shh . . . shh . . . shh . . .*"
Norbert hissed at my ear.

My father came in with a tray
and the appetizer plates.
"Having a good time?"

Norbert and I looked at each other.

Father carried a tureen of soup on the tray
back to the dining room.

Norbert stared at his dinner
as if it were
a nest of germs from outer space.
"We eat frozen glop
in the kitchen
while they eat like kings
in the dining room."
With the handle of his fork,

Norbert poked holes
in his mashed potatoes.
One by one, he buried his peas
in the holes.
Over their graves,
he spooned the juice
from his apple compote.
All the while,
he insulted my parents
and our kitchen
and even the place mats.

Mother came in with soup plates
and smiled, without really looking at us.
"Having fun, boys?"
She took the salads to the dining room.

Norbert floated apple slices
in his gravy.
"Why is a grumpy old dog
in there with the grown-ups,
while we get stuck in the kitchen
with cheap frozen dinners?"

"Don't say anything
about Mrs. Tree or her dog,"
I told him nervously.
"She's scary."

"You are dumb.
Dumb, dumb, dumb."
Tearing his napkin into bits,
he scattered them over his dinner.

My father came in with the salad plates.
"How's it going, guys?"

He took everything from the oven,
and put it on the tray,
and carried it to the dining room.

"What do you want to bet
that dog is eating with them?"
Norbert poured salt
over his place mat.
"Pickles," he snapped.
"We don't even get pickles.
How do they expect us to eat this junk,
if they don't even give us a pickle?"
Pushing back his chair,
he stomped to the refrigerator
and opened the door.
"I don't even see . . .
Wow! Look at that pie!"

"Don't touch it!"
I hurried to the refrigerator.
"My father made it."

"Nobody would notice
if we took a little . . ."

"Norbert, if you touch that pie
I'll yell bloody murder."

I could see he thought
I just might do it,
but he wasn't willing
to back down completely.
"There's the pickle jar,
behind the pie."
He started to reach
toward the back of the shelf.

"Wait."

If I knew Norbert,
he would manage to accidentally
drag his sleeve across the pie,
or drop the pickle jar on it.
I also knew
that if I did yell bloody murder
or anything else
during this fancy dinner party
I would get in trouble,
and, somehow, Norbert would not.
If I went in and announced
that he was threatening the pie,
I would be the tattletale,
whose whining
meant my mother did not have
a civilized family.
I grabbed Norbert's wrist.
"Just *wait.*"

Not even breathing,
I lifted that beautiful,
shimmery, soft heavy pie
out of the refrigerator.
"Now get your pickles."

Norbert took out the jar.
"DILL PICKLES!"

"Quiet!"
I was terrified one of my parents
would find me holding that pie.

"I hate dill pickles," Norbert stormed.
"Dill pickles taste like swamp weeds."

"Put them back, then."
I promised myself
that if I could only get this pie
safely back on the shelf
without my parents knowing
I'd touched it,
I would never do anything
wrong or dumb or sloppy again.

Norbert took a pickle from the jar
and ate it.
"Ugh! Yuck! Ick! Horrible!"
He took another pickle,
then put the jar back in the refrigerator
and turned to me.
"Hey. Look. There's a fly on the pie."

He was right.
A fly had landed
right in the middle
of that glorious cream pie.

Norbert scrunched up his face.
"*Eeyew. Eeyew. Fly* germs!"

I knew that if my mother or father
came in and saw me
holding the pie with a fly on it,
the rest of my life
would not be worth living.
Carefully, I took my hand
from under the pie plate
and waved it at the fly,
whispering, "Shoo! Shoo!"

"Hey!" Norbert said.
"Now you've got a shoo fly pie."

The fly refused to flee.
I wondered if he might be
stuck in the thick gooey topping.

"Swat it," Norbert suggested.

I shook my head.
I did not want to kill a fly.
I especially did not want to kill
a fly on my father's cream pie.
Besides, I could imagine
how a swatted cream pie would look.

Norbert handed me
an empty plastic glass.
"Put this over it, then."

"*Why?*"

"That's how you trap flies
on paper."

Desperate, I popped the glass,
upside down, over the fly.

That fly was furious.
It began buzzing like a power saw,
or a model airplane.
I heard my father's voice
in the dining room.
"Is everyone ready for dessert?"

"Now what?" I asked Norbert frantically.

"Well, if the fly were on paper,
you'd turn everything over
so the paper would be on top.
Then you'd have the fly trapped in the glass.
Too bad the pie isn't paper."

I thought I heard chairs
being scraped back
in the dining room.

With my left hand on the glass,
I tilted the plate a little,
hoping the fly might fall into the glass.

"It's not turned enough, dummy."
Norbert nudged one side of the pie plate up,
too hard
and too far.

Floop.
All the pie filling
except for the part under the glass
slid out of the shell.

"Oops," Norbert said,
in a very, *very* sincere voice.
We looked at the lemon cream on my foot.
"Now you have a fly pie shoe."

"*YOU!*"

We looked up.
My father seemed taller
than I remembered him.

"*You!*"

Very carefully,
I put the pie plate
on the kitchen counter.

Seizing my arm,
my father kept his voice low and savage.
"I'll deal with you later.
Right now, you clean that mess
off the floor.
What is that buzzing?"

"A fly under the glass Philip put
on the pie," Norbert said politely.

My father shook my arm.
"You are demented," he told me.
"Hopeless. Beyond cure."
He looked around the kitchen.
"Norbert, pick the best looking fruit
from that bowl."
His hands shaking, my father
took some cheese from the refrigerator
and sliced it.
He arranged cheese slices on a platter,
with the fruit in the middle,
and took it back to the dining room.

As I wiped lemon cream off the floor,
Norbert lifted the glass
off the pie shell.
"Oops! The pie fly flew."

I heard Mrs. Tree in the dining room.
"Fruit and cheese?
What a tasteful dessert.
I can never understand people
who top off a lovely meal
with sweet gooey pies or cakes.
It's so tacky to stuff guests with
cakes and pies—all sugar and calories."

Norbert chased the fly
until he lost interest in it.
I wiped my shoes
and the floor
and cleared the kitchen table.

When Norbert heard my mother coming,
he started brushing crumbs off the place mats.
"It's nice of you to help, Norbert," Mother said.
"You boys may go into the parlor
and say good night now,
and then go to bed."

Remembering how Mrs. Tree had looked at me,
I had a horrible feeling
she might even know
what had happened with the pie.

As I went into the parlor,
lagging a little behind Norbert,
the dog leaped off Mrs. Tree's lap
and ran at me.
Before I could move,
it started licking my shoes.

"Look at that!" Mrs. Tree said.
"Kong never makes up to strangers,
and he has absolutely no use for children!
What a remarkable boy!
Kong simply adores him."

"*That* dog is named Kong?" Norbert asked.

Glancing up from my shoe,
Kong snarled at him.

"Bedtime, boys."
Father put his hands
firmly on Norbert's shoulder and mine.

Mrs. Tree smiled at me
and told me I would have to come visit
Kong and her soon.

As Norbert and I left the room,
she told my parents,
"You know, you can never fool a dog.
That other boy, now,
definitely has a shifty look."

As we got ready for bed,
Norbert growled, "Dumb dog.
If I'd knocked the pie on *my* shoe
she would have thought it loved *me*.
Oh! Hi, Uncle Mort."

My father stood in the doorway.
"Norbert, I think it's more than your look
that is shifty.
I have a strong feeling, Norbert,
from what you just said,
that you murdered my lemon cream pie.
Do you know how I feel
about my pies, Norbert?
Do you know how I feel about people
who attack my pies?
From now on, Norbert,
I will be watching you!"

When my father left,
Norbert crawled into bed.
"He can't talk to me like that!
It's the last time I come over here
to keep *you* company!"

I was asleep
when a loud buzzing woke me.
Getting out of bed,
I unhooked my window screen
and held it open.
I thought that fly would never leave,
but how could I refuse to help him out?
It might have been the fly
that showed Mrs. Tree
my parents had taste, and style,
and a civilized child that no dog could resist.

BEVERLY KELLER "gives us an under-the-skin sense of a kid alone," said *Kirkus Reviews*, commenting on FIONA'S FLEA, the sequel to her first book, FIONA'S BEE, which was starred by *Booklist*, *Kirkus Reviews*, and *School Library Journal*.

Other popular books she's written include THE BEETLE BUSH, described as "funny and feeling" when starred by *School Library Journal*, and THE SEA WATCH, called "a madcap mystery" by *Kirkus Reviews*.

A friend to all animals, the author shares her home in Davis, California, with five large but lovable dogs.

BOBBY LEWIS recently finished the drawings for her first picture book, THE HOUSE THAT JACK BUILT. Originally from Texas, where her work has been exhibited in such galleries as A Clean Well-Lighted Place, she holds an M.F.A. from Pratt Institute.

The artist now lives in New York City with her cat, Nacho.